There's a
Dragon About

THERE'S A DRAGON ABOUT

A WINTER'S REVEL

BY RICHARD AND
RONI SCHOTTER

ILLUSTRATED BY

R. W. ALLEY

ORCHARD BOOKS
NEW YORK

This text is adapted from
the Oxfordshire St. George play.

Text copyright © 1994 by Richard Schotter and Roni Schotter
Illustrations copyright © 1994 by R. W. Alley

Orchard Books
95 Madison Avenue
New York, NY 10016

Manufactured in the United States of America
Printed by Barton Press, Inc.
Bound by Horowitz/Rae
Book design by R. W. Alley and Sylvia Frezzolini
The text of this book is set in 16 point Palatino.
The illustrations are pen-and-ink drawings with watercolors.

10 9 8 7 6 5 4 3 2 1

Library of Congress Cataloging-in-Publication Data
Schotter, Richard.   There's a dragon about : a winter's revel / by
Richard and Roni Schotter ; illustrated by R. W. Alley.   p.   cm.
"This text is adapted from the Oxfordshire St. George play"—T.p.
verso.
Summary: King Cole, Queen Meg, Jack, Tess, Giant Blunderbore,
and Sir George battle a ferocious dragon.
   ISBN 0-531-06858-7. — ISBN 0-531-08708-5 (lib. bdg.)
[1. Dragons—Fiction.   2. Stories in rhyme.]   I. Schotter, Roni.
II. Alley, R. W. (Robert W.), ill.   III. Title.
PZ8.3.S375Th   1994   93-46421
[E]—dc20

To the Strums—
    Kate, Alec, Chuck, and Becky—
       for holiday revels past and present,
and to Jesse
       for future revels all year round
                —R.S. & R.S.

To Paige Gillies
      —R.W.A.

Hold, friends, hold! We are very cold.

Inside and outside, we are very cold.

Something to warm us, if we may.

For that, kind folks, we'll give you a play.

There's a dragon about.
If you see him, shout!
He grunts.
   He groans.
      He growls.
         He grins.
Watch!
Our revel now begins.

I'm King Cole,
and here is my bride.
I've a crown on my head
and a sword by my side.

I'm Queen Meg.
Hear what I say.
I'm scared of dragons,
but I won't run away.

Jack's my name.
I'm brave as can be.
I can kill dragons.
They're nothing to me.

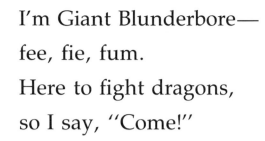

I'm Giant Blunderbore—
fee, fie, fum.
Here to fight dragons,
so I say, "Come!"

The dragon I'll battle
without any fear,
but show me a giant,
and I disappear.

Come on out, little man Jack.

A thump on your rump and a whack on your back.

My name's Tess,
full five years old,
ready to battle
the dragon bold.

So here we join and take our stand,
Blunderbore, brave Tess, and Jack at hand.
If you see the dragon, ring a bell,
clap your hands, or give a yell.

Stand on head, stand on feet!
Meat! Meat!
   Meat for to eat!
I am the Dragon—
   here are my jaws!
I am the Dragon—
   here are my claws!
Meat! Meat!
   Meat for to eat!
Stand on head, stand on feet.

I am George, the famous knight.
What can we use to win this fight?

These are our tricks—
ho, Dragon, ho!
These are our sticks—
whack, Dragon, so!

Ho!
Ho!
Ho!
Whack, Dragon, so!

Look, my friends, they've fallen down.
Can someone raise them from the ground?

I am the doctor. I cure all ills.
Not with potions, not with pills.
I cure itch, stitch, pox, and gout,
pains within and pains without.
I'll cast a spell and wave my hand,
and order everyone to stand.

Like winter's end when spring rains fall,
Nature, be freed and heed my call.
Bloom again, rise again, one and all!

Get up, King. Wake up, Bride.
Tess, Jack, George, stand aside.
Up from the floor, Blunderbore!
The dreadful Dragon is no more.
All rejoice, girl and boy,
and wish the people winter joy.

Hey! What about me?
I've been bad, no doubt.
But must I lie here lonely,
all left out?

Dragons stay dead in stories of old.

But we agree to break that mold.

Rise up, Dragon, and kindly greet us.

We forgive you now,

though you tried to eat us.

Put up your sticks.
An end to the fun.
Stop all your tricks.
Our revel is done.

Be there loaf in your locker,
and sheep in your fold,
a fire on your hearth,
and good luck for your lot,
money in your pocket,
and a pudding in your pot!

Hold, friends, hold! We are very cold.

Inside and outside, we are very cold.

Something to warm us, if we may.

For that, kind folks, we'll give you a play.

Many years ago, before there were televisions or radios, revels, like the one the children in this book put on, were performed during the winter holiday season by ordinary people who traveled from house to house to entertain their neighbors. These winter revellers made their own costumes out of simple materials such as paper and cardboard. Sometimes they even used frying pans for hats.

You and your friends can be revellers too and act out this revel at home, in school, or anywhere. You can make your own swords, crowns, and costumes. Each of you can play a single role or you might take turns playing more than one part. Here are the names of the characters, the *Dramatis Personae*.

DRAMATIS PERSONAE

Narrator	Brave Tess
King Cole	Dragon
Queen Meg	Knight George
Little Jack	Doctor
Giant Blunderbore